Life can sure change fast! Mine did. And all because Mom went on a vacation by her-self. The problem wasn't the vacation. The problem was that she returned with more than a suntan. Much more! She came home with a new husband. And the new husband had three kids!

Talk about shocked! You never saw three people more shocked than my sister, Karen, my brother, Mark, and me (I'm Dana). The new husband's three kids weren't too thrilled, either. It was deep dislike at first sight.

But you know what? We're slowly getting to be a real family. It hasn't been easy, though. So I thought I'd do my part to help. I found a bunch of pictures and I decided to put them together in our very first family album. None of the pictures are too old because … well, because we're a brand-new family. But, hey, everybody's got to start somewhere.

Carol

I'll start with my mom. She's pretty great—organized, smart, and funny. She's so sensible that I'd never have thought she'd fall in love and get married so quickly. She did, though. I guess there are sides to her personality I'll just never understand.

Frank

And here's the man of Mom's dreams: Frank Lambert, my new stepdad. At first I thought he was such a geek. Don't tell anyone I said this, but now I think Frank is actually fairly cool. A little disorganized and goofy, but cool.

The Gangs All Here

And here's our new family! Starting with Frank and going clockwise: that's Frank's son J.T.; his daughter, Al (short for Alicia); his son Brendan; Mom; my brother, Mark; my sister, Karen; and me.

Love at First Sight—Not!

The first time we met Frank's kids was at our barbecue. Things did *not* go well. No one even knew Mom and Frank were married yet. Before they could tell us, the barbecue turned into an angry food fight.

I couldn't believe what brats Frank's kids were. I think even Mom was having second thoughts that day.

Frank was so tense that he set the grill on fire. His son J.T.'s hamburger was *super* well done, to put it mildly.

Good News...Bad News!

All the kids had a fit when Mom and Frank announced they had gotten married. It wasn't exactly the happy moment Mom had hoped for. She felt rotten. Frank convinced her to hang in there.

I was horrified that Frank and his family were coming to live with us. I called all my friends for help, but no one had any ideas on how to stop it from happening.

My sister, Karen, wasn't happy, either. I didn't really expect her to come up with any brilliant ideas, though. She's the beauty, and I'm the brains. And *I* didn't know what to do.

Finally I told Mom how I felt. She understood, but she asked for my help. I could see that making this work was really super-important to her.

Karen and I suddenly became closer. It used to be that we had nothing in common. She's extremely into fashion and very vain about her good looks. But suddenly we had one big thing in common: We both wanted Frank Lambert and his kids to disappear!

Move-in Day!

Finally the big day came. Frank and his family arrived loaded down with all their stuff. Boy, did they have stuff! We stood on our porch and wondered how they would ever cram all of it inside our house.

Frank gave his kids a real stern talking-to before they came into the house. From the looks on their faces, they were dreading living with us as much as we dreaded living with them.

J.T. and I immediately tried to stare each other down, but neither of us would give in. And neither of us liked what we were looking at.

When Al unpacked her pet pig, I thought my entire family would faint!

In fact, my little brother, Mark, did faint. I didn't blame him. It was a lot to deal with.

Mealtime!

Blending families isn't easy—especially when you're trying to blend a neat, orderly family (mine) with a slob family (theirs). Mom insisted that we wait for them and eat as a family. We nearly starved to death waiting.

When they finally did show up, Al brought her pig, and J.T. wanted to eat in the living room. There was no family dinner. I was *so* annoyed that we'd had to wait for nothing.

But I was not half as annoyed then as I was when J.T. threw spaghetti at me. And all because I merely implied that he had a lower IQ than Al's pig and worse manners. Some people are *so* sensitive!

Even Frank knew his son was out of control. I mean, who squirts choco-late syrup right into his mouth? Sometimes it seemed that J.T. was trying to gross us out on purpose.

Even though Brendan, J.T., and Al never made it to the table at meal-
times, they weren't exactly starving. They raided the refrigerator constant-
ly. Here they are, wolfing down the last of the avocado dip. But I came
along and told them it was really Karen's avocado cold-cream pack. Ha!

This was a typical school morning at the Lambert household—total
chaos! Here Brendan, Al, and J.T. rip apart cereal boxes, probably search-
ing madly for prizes. I'm telling you, those kids were animals!

And Then Came ... Cody!

Besides Frank's three kids, Cody also came to live with us. He's Frank's nephew. What a space case! "Like, awesome, dude" is his favorite expression. Not exactly brain surgeon material, yet every once in a while he comes out with something unexpectedly smart.

Mom to the Rescue??

With the chaos created by all the different personalities under one roof, Mom and Frank knew they were in trouble. Something had to be done. But what?

When the going gets tough, Mom makes lists. So one night she stayed up almost all night making lists of rules for the household. Mom was sure the rules would solve all our problems. Frank had his doubts.

The very next day Mom called our first family meeting. It was to explain all her new rules. She'd made up charts and everything. Sometimes Mom carries her love of organization a little too far.

When Mark learned he'd be sharing laundry duty with Al, he was worried. He probably thought Al would hang *him* up to dry. I think Frank was concerned about the same thing.

For the first time, *all* the kids agreed on something. We all hated Mom's new rules. The rules were so strict, we felt like we were in jail. We complained to Frank, but he took Mom's side. He told us all to try our best.

Al was the one who had the hardest time with the new rules. She's a tomboy and a definite individual. She likes doing things her *own* way. She couldn't believe her ears when she heard the rules.

Karen and I tried to observe the rules about when to study and when to watch TV, but Al wouldn't. The whole idea upset her so much that she decided to run away!

Mom caught up with her before she was able to leave. They had a long talk. Mom told Al that she was sorry the rules made her so unhappy. Al told Mom that some of the rules were okay, but that others were real dumb. Mom listened and promised to give Al's suggestions a lot of thought.

The Family That Plays Together...

Mom announced to the family that she was rethinking her rules. Poor Mom. She was trying so hard. It wasn't easy for her.

Then Frank came up with *his* big idea for family togetherness—a camping trip! That seemed like an even worse idea than Mom's rules!

The camping trip was a disaster right from the start. We couldn't even agree on which *direction* to go in!

No one in my family is the outdoors type. Mark was scared to death of seeing a snake. The bugs were bugging me—and so was Frank. He kept telling us how much fun we would be having ... over and over and over again.

Karen fretted the whole time about breaking her nails. I spent my time begging Mom to take us home. Why sleep on the hard ground when you have a bed at home? The whole thing made no sense to me.

Something good happened, though. J.T. was really nice to Mark. They actually started acting like brothers! So maybe braving the bugs was worth it after all.

I was starting to see J.T. in a different light. He wasn't the animal I thought he was. Not totally, anyway. In fact, he's capable of being very sweet when he wants to be.

Musical Madness

When Al formed a rock band, Mom and Frank were supportive. Even Karen and I were dragged into being backup singers. But we never expected J.T. to get involved the way he did. He volunteered to be the band's manager, though he wound up doing much more than that.

At the group's very first job, half the singers couldn't make it. So J.T. and Cody dressed as girls and went on for them. Unfortunately, their disguises didn't fool the club's owner.

Thank goodness Mom was there. She jumped in and stopped the customers from leaving by belting out a song. The crowd loved her, and the gig was saved.

Although the evening was nearly a disaster, it was great for Al. She saw that her entire family was there for her. She told J.T. he was the greatest big brother in the world.

Coming Together

J.T. wasn't the only one I was seeing a new side of. There was also turning out to be more to Cody than I'd thought. (Even though both of them still mess up Mom's clean floor without a second thought, as they are about to do in this photo.)

I remember one time when Cody bailed me out of a tight spot. He did it even after I'd been really snotty to him. Here I am making fun of his guitar-playing and a song he'd written. Boy, did I feel bad about it after what happened later....

I sneaked out to a really seedy bar to see a folksinger I liked. Cody came down to make sure I was all right and wound up having to defend me from a bunch of creepy goons. He didn't want to fight, but when he was forced to, he was awesome! I was impressed—and very grateful.

Then Mom and Frank showed up to help us out. By the time the fight was over, even the folksinger was scared of us. Wow! What a family!

Getting Real

I guess we've all had a rough road with this "new" family. It's getting smoother, though. I really think of Brendan as my baby brother now. *Somebody's* got to be on his side when Mom and Frank get to be too much for him. (Like in *this* photo.)

J.T. and I are getting along. Not all the time, of course. But that's okay. Real brothers and sisters fight sometimes, too. The important thing is that we know we're there for one another.

Al has also settled in. She's got her band, her Little League, and her pig—and her family behind her. She's starting to feel better about everything.

She's growing up, too. She actually wore a dress to her school dance! For her, that's unbelievable. She wasn't sure if she wanted to dance until her pal Urkel showed up and got everyone going.

To me, this photo shows how my new family started out—just Mom and Frank trying to go it alone and pull a family together.

This photo shows how it's turning out. We're all one family, pulling together and helping each other out.

Not only are we pulling together, but we're having a ball doing it. When Karen and Al can laugh together, you *know* things are going well.

We're working together…

…and we're starting to feel like winners.

Step by step, we're winning at becoming a family. And the truth is, it feels great!